A YOU-DRAW-IT STORY

~Clyde~
the Curly-Furred Mouse

Written by C. C. Vaughan

Illustrated by _____

Clyde
the Curly-Furred Mouse

Written by C. C. Vaughan

Illustrated by _____

An Imprint of
Castlebrook Publications

ISBN 978-0-9798242-3-4

Castlebrook Publications
1535 Farmers Lane, PMB#237
Santa Rosa, CA 95405
www.youdrawitbooks.com

Clyde is a very unusual mouse. He is the only mouse in the world with curly fur.

Clyde

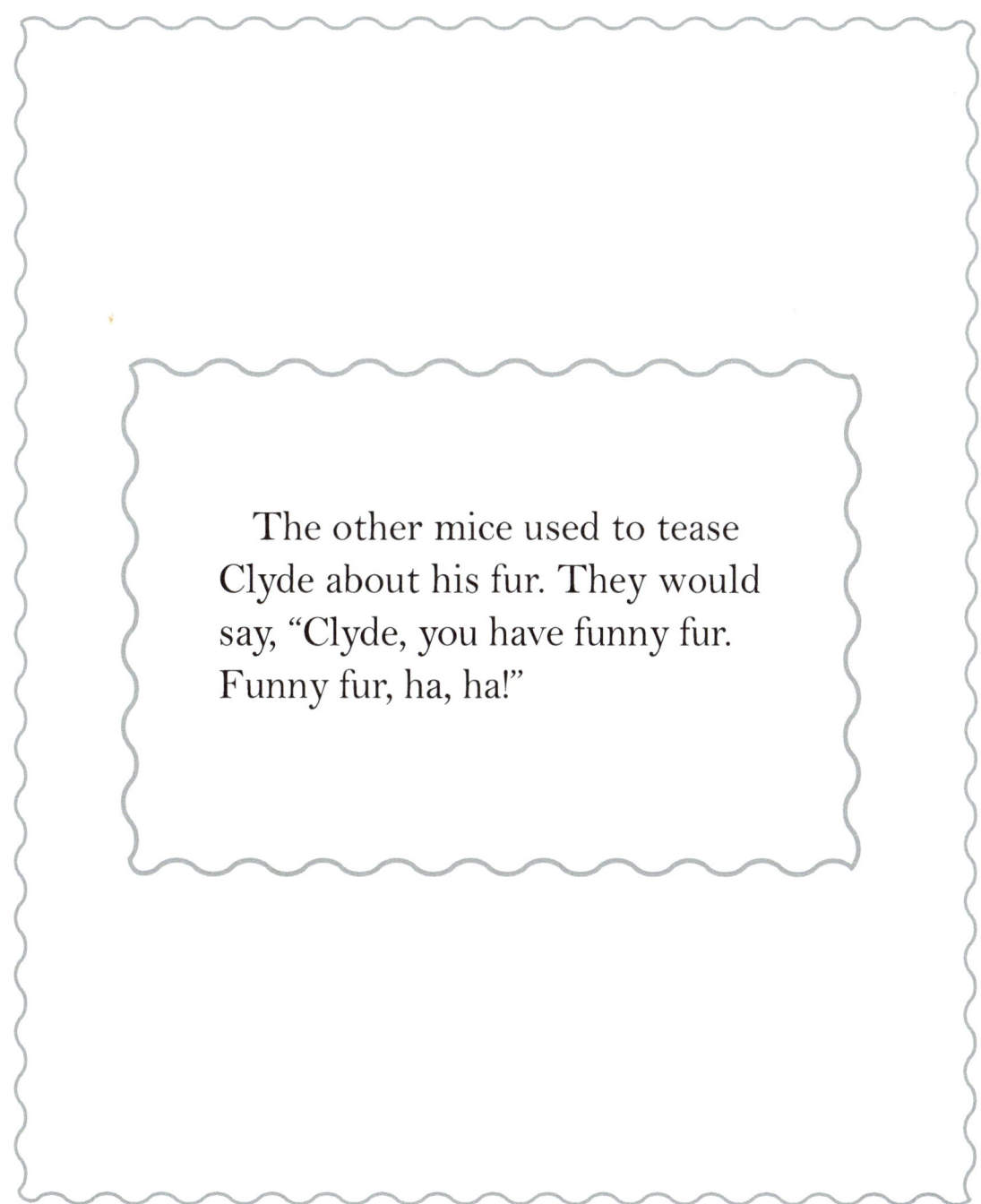

The other mice used to tease Clyde about his fur. They would say, "Clyde, you have funny fur. Funny fur, ha, ha!"

The Laughing Mice

"You look like a sheep!"

"You look like a poodle!"

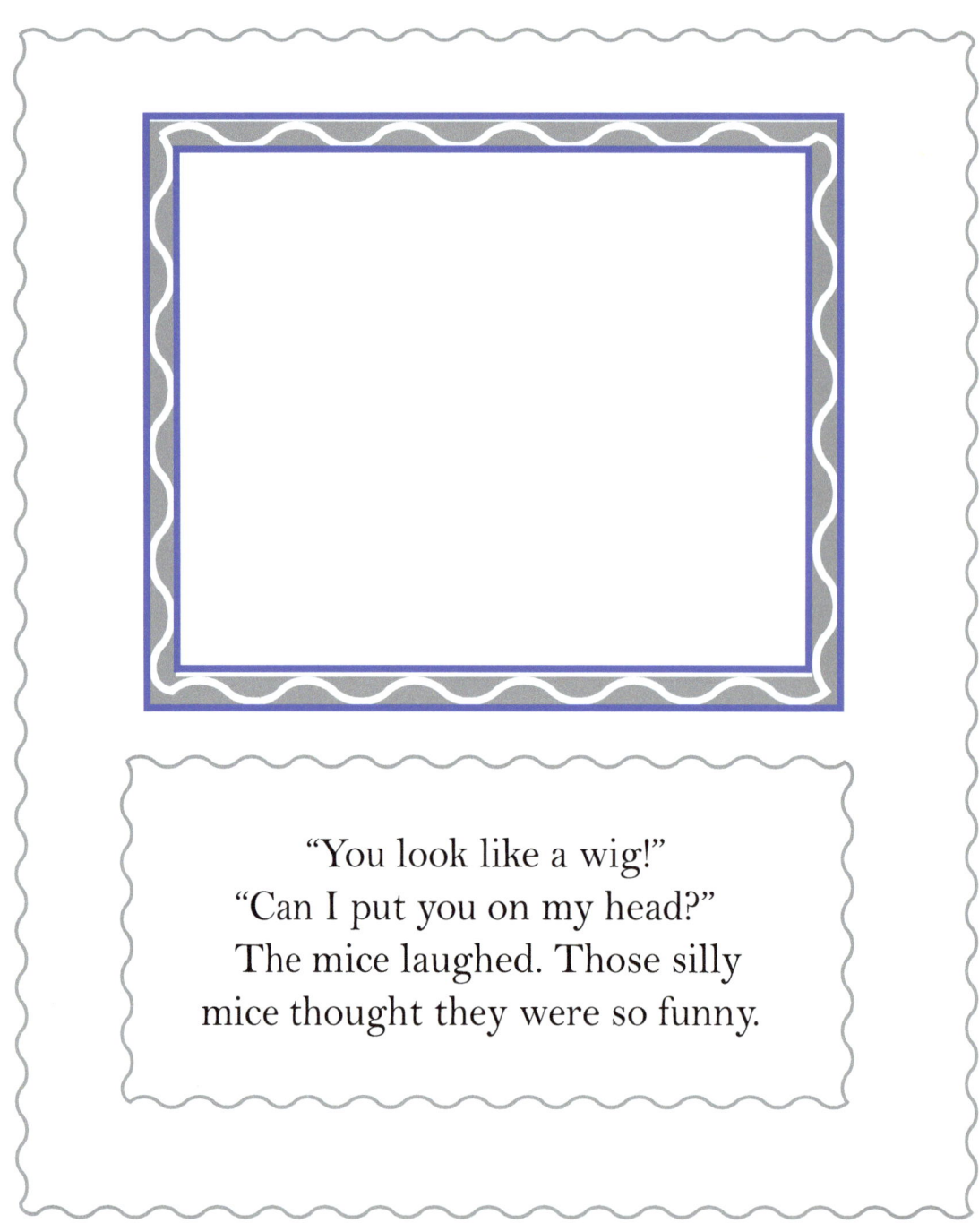

"You look like a wig!"
"Can I put you on my head?"
The mice laughed. Those silly
mice thought they were so funny.

Clyde didn't let their mean words bother him. He replied, "My curly fur is thicker than yours. It will keep me warm this winter."

The other mice said, "Who needs it? We'll be warm enough, ha, ha, ha!"

Winter came very soon. It was the coldest winter in a hundred years. The little mice shivered and shook in the cold North Wind. Now, instead of "Ha, ha, ha," they all said, "B-r-r-r, b-r-r, b-r-r-r."

The Mice in the Snow

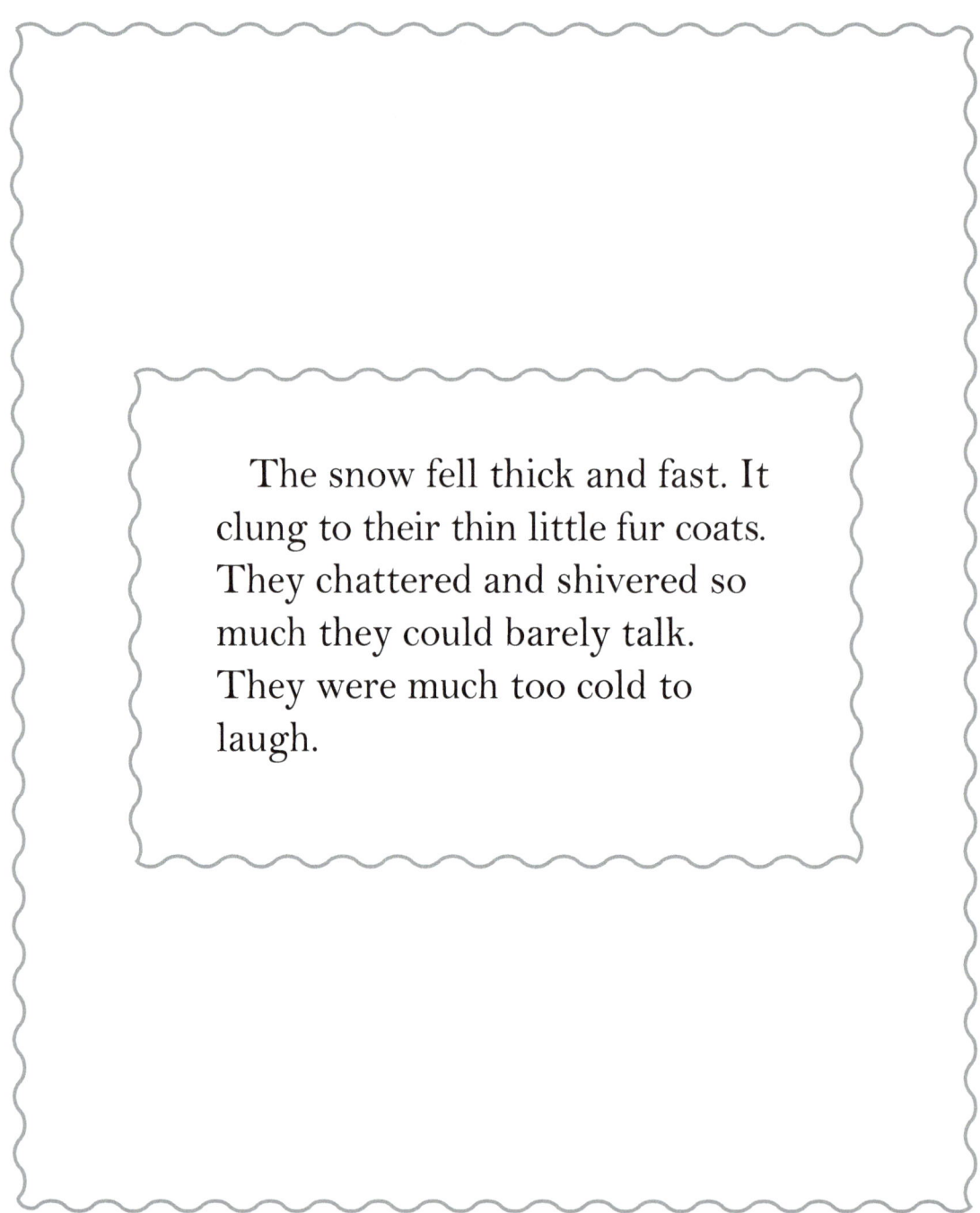

The snow fell thick and fast. It clung to their thin little fur coats. They chattered and shivered so much they could barely talk. They were much too cold to laugh.

"C-C-C-Clyde," they chattered, their tiny teeth clicking together as they shivered.

"C-C-C-Clyde! We're so c-c-c-cold! What sh-sh-shall we do?"

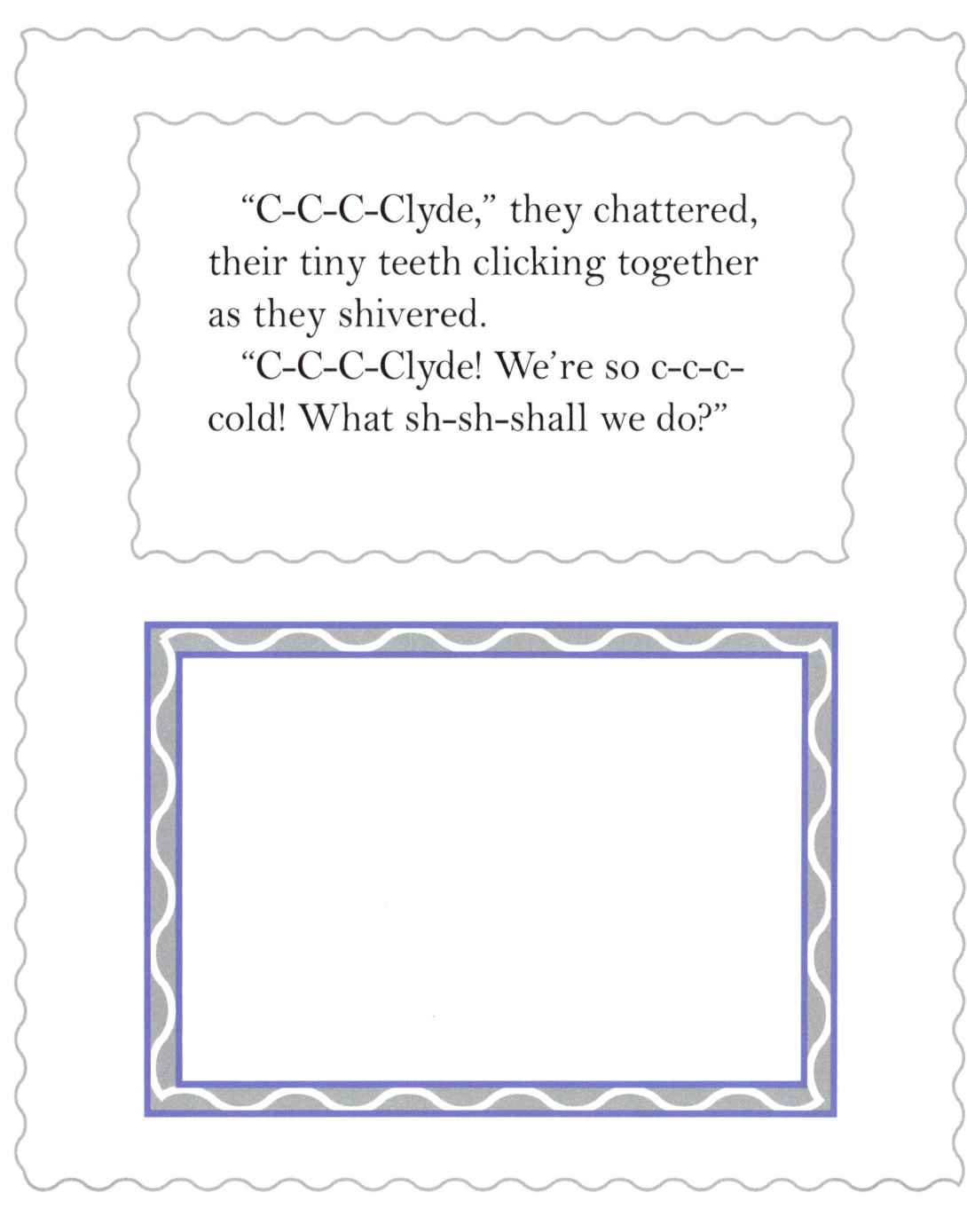

Clyde thought for a moment. "I remember you said I looked like a sheep. That gives me an idea."

So, off Clyde went to the sheep pen. He said to the sheep, "My friends are very cold this winter. Do you have any wool you can spare for coats?"

The sheep said, "Baa, baa, baa, yes, we do." They happily set about making tiny, curly-furred coats out of wool for all the mice,

The Sheep Sew Little Coats

Clyde Wears His New Hat

except for Clyde, that is. He already had plenty of curly fur.

One of the sheep said, "Clyde, you don't need a coat, but I want to make something for you, too, so I will make you a tiny hat to keep your ears warm."

The other sheep thought the tiny

little hat was so cute that they made little hats for all the other mice.

Clyde carried the coats and hats home to his friends. The shivering little mice gladly put on the curly-furred coats. They laughed with glee at how warm they felt.

Then they put on the tiny curly-furred hats. Clyde looked at them and laughed. "Now you all look like tiny sheep wearing wigs! Ha, ha, ha!"

The Mice in Their New Hats and Coats

The little mice all looked at each other and burst out laughing.

"Thank you Clyde," they said. "You look like a sheep, too. You were smart to think of these warm coats for us. We're all so glad you have curly fur, Clyde, and a curly brain, too, Ha, ha, ha!"

"Clever, curly Clyde. Curly clever Clyde. Ha, ha, ha!"

Then the little mice scampered off to thank the sheep and show them how funny they could be.

The Mice and the Sheep

INTEGRATING ART AND
WHOLE LANGUAGE DEVELOPMENT

YOU-DRAW-IT BOOKS are excellent learning tools. They integrate art and whole language to help children build comprehension skills. These books are interactive and stimulate the mind of the child to respond to the stories with drawings. The books are of particular interest to reluctant readers. One mother said that her 10-year-old daughter hates to read, but loves to draw. They have a reading session every day. When the book *The Girl Who Lived with Rabbits* was introduced in the reading time, the girl would read nothing else. She became eager for reading time rather than reluctant.

The stories are fun and are written to make the student think about virtues such as caring, truth, character, and the inner self. The child's natural tendency to draw is allowed to become part of the story, utilizing the learning relationship, which many teachers try to develop.

Five and six-year olds who can't read yet enjoy the books just as much as readers. They can't wait to draw the pictures of the shorter books after you read them the story. This is a great opportunity for the parent to interact with a child on a project.

MORE YOU-DRAWIT-BOOKS

There's a Pig in the Firehouse! — 5-8
The Tale of Artie's Tail — 5-8
The Girl Who Lived with Rabbits — 5-10
Artie Goes to Hollywood 8-12
More coming soon

www.ingramcontent.com/pod-product-compliance
Lightning Source LLC
Chambersburg PA
CBHW041010170626
46815CB00002B/236